Action

Alphabet

Shelley Rotner

Athenuem Books for Young Readers
An imprint of Simon & Schuster Children's Publishing Division
1230 Avenue of the Americas, New York, New York 10020

Book design by Michael Nelson

The text for this book is set in Futura.

Manufactured in the United States of America

First edition
10 9 8 7 6 5 4 3 2 1

Library of Congress Cataloging-in-Publication Data
Rotner, Shelley.
        Action alphabet / by Shelley Rotner. — 1st ed.
        p.   cm.
        ISBN 0-689-80086-X
        1. English language — Alphabet — Juvenile literature.   I. Title.
PE1155.R68   1996
421'.1 — dc20   94-32212

For the children
—S. R.

Arching

Blowing

Climbing

Diving

Eating

Floating

Giggling

Hugging

Ice skating

Juggling

Kicking

Leaping

Mowing

Napping

Opening

Painting

Quilting

Running

Swinging

Tugging

Undressing

Vacuuming

Waving

X-ing

Yawning

Zipping